To Vinson,
a boy who makes
the best dumplings.
— Y.C.C.

To my mom, dad,
and sister.
—J.Y.

immedium

Immedium, Inc.
P.O. Box 31846, San Francisco, CA 94131
www.immedium.com

First hardcover edition published 2009 by Holiday House.
First Immedium hardcover edition published 2016.

This book was typeset with Contra, Adobe Fansong Std, American Typewriter, Cronos Pro, and Adobe Kaiti Std.
The illustrations were created with watercolor and gouache on paper.

Book design by Dorothy Mak
Chinese translation by Xiaoqing Chen and Carissa Duan
中文审校: 张瀛 , 邹海燕

Printed in Malaysia
10 9 8 7 6 5 4 3 2 1

Library of Congress Cataloging-in-Publication Data

Compestine, Ying Chang.
  Boy Dumplings / by Ying Chang Compestine ; illustrated by James Yamasaki. — 1st ed.
    p. cm.
  Summary: When a hungry ghost threatens to gobble up a plump little boy,
  the boy tricks the ghost by convincing him to prepare an elaborate recipe first.
  ISBN-13: 978-0-8234-1955-5
  [1. Ghosts — Fiction. 2. Cookery — Fiction. 3. China — Fiction]
  I. Yamasaki, James, ill. II. Title: PZ7.C7 3615Boy 2009
  [E] — dc22

2006050064

ISBN: 978-1-59702-119-7

BOY DUMPLINGS

A Tasty Chinese Tale

男孩馅饺子:中国美食故事

By

Ying Chang Compestine

Illustrated by

James Yamasaki

immedium
San Francisco, Ca

张瀛 / 文
山崎博 / 图

In Beijing, the capital of China, there once lived a tall, skinny ghost. He believed that only foolish ghosts work hard for their meals.

This smart ghost simply strolled through streets at night, collecting the offerings of food that people left him in big buckets. Then, one night, the offerings stopped.

在中国的京城，北京，住着一个又瘦又高的鬼。他认为只有傻鬼才会为一日三餐劳累奔波。

这个自认聪明的鬼每天夜里满街游荡，收集人们留在桶里的贡物。然而，一天晚上，鬼发现人们不再给他留贡物了。

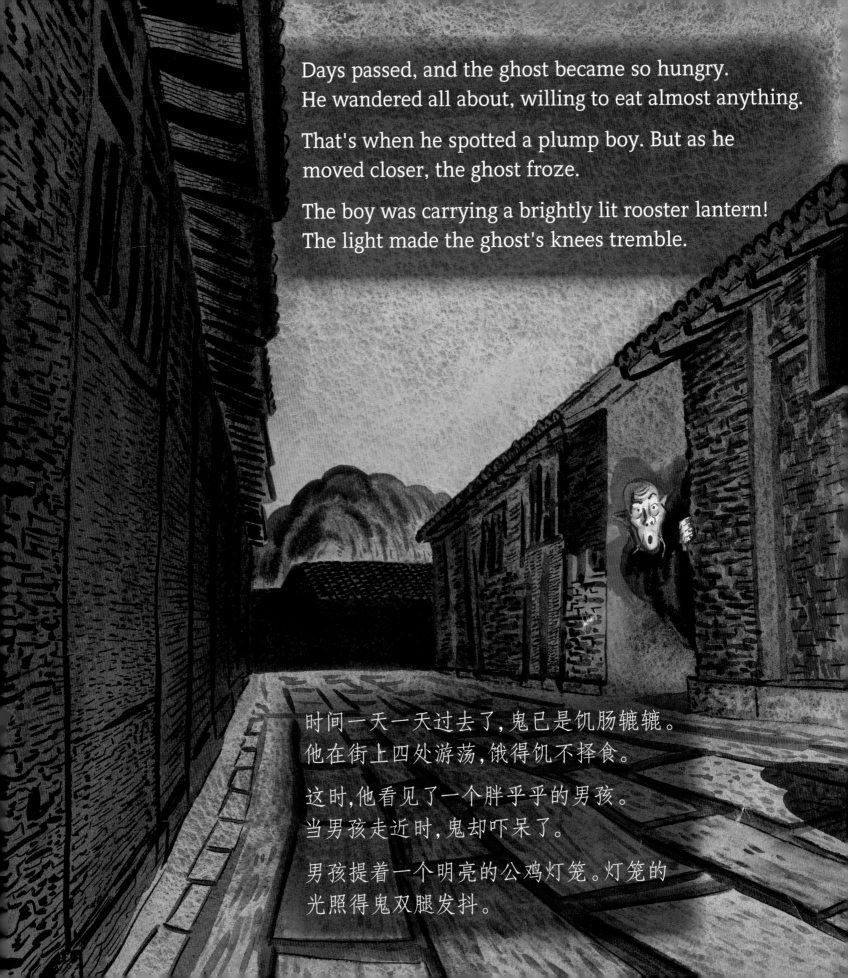

Days passed, and the ghost became so hungry.
He wandered all about, willing to eat almost anything.

That's when he spotted a plump boy. But as he
moved closer, the ghost froze.

The boy was carrying a brightly lit rooster lantern!
The light made the ghost's knees tremble.

时间一天一天过去了，鬼已是饥肠辘辘。
他在街上四处游荡，饿得饥不择食。

这时，他看见了一个胖乎乎的男孩。
当男孩走近时，鬼却吓呆了。

男孩提着一个明亮的公鸡灯笼。灯笼的
光照得鬼双腿发抖。

The ghost could hardly believe his luck when the boy's lantern suddenly flickered out. He grabbed him.

"Let me go!" cried the boy. "Oh, pyew! You must be the Garbage-Eating Ghost."

"Garbage!" the ghost roared. "I only eat delectable treats!"

"Like me?" asked the boy.

"Yes!" the ghost giggled.

突然，男孩的灯笼熄灭了。鬼没有想到自己会这么走运，他一把抓住了男孩。

"放开我！"男孩大叫着。"噢！真臭，你一定是那个吃垃圾的鬼。"

"垃圾！"鬼大吼起来，"我只吃美味佳肴。"

"像我一样美味吗？"男孩问道。

"是的！"鬼咯咯地笑起来。

The ghost carried the boy to his house. Once inside, he fetched a bucket and a pair of chopsticks. "You're not going to eat me raw, are you?" asked the boy.

鬼把男孩带回了家。一进门，鬼就拿来饭桶和筷子。"你不会生吃我吧？"男孩问道。

"Of course," answered the ghost.

"I know a delicious recipe for boy dumplings," said the boy.

"I love dumplings," cried the ghost. "Give me the recipe!" So the boy did.

"当然会啦,"鬼答道。

"我知道怎么做美味男孩馅饺子,"男孩说。

"我最喜欢吃饺子了。"鬼叫道,"快告诉我!"于是男孩慢慢讲起来。

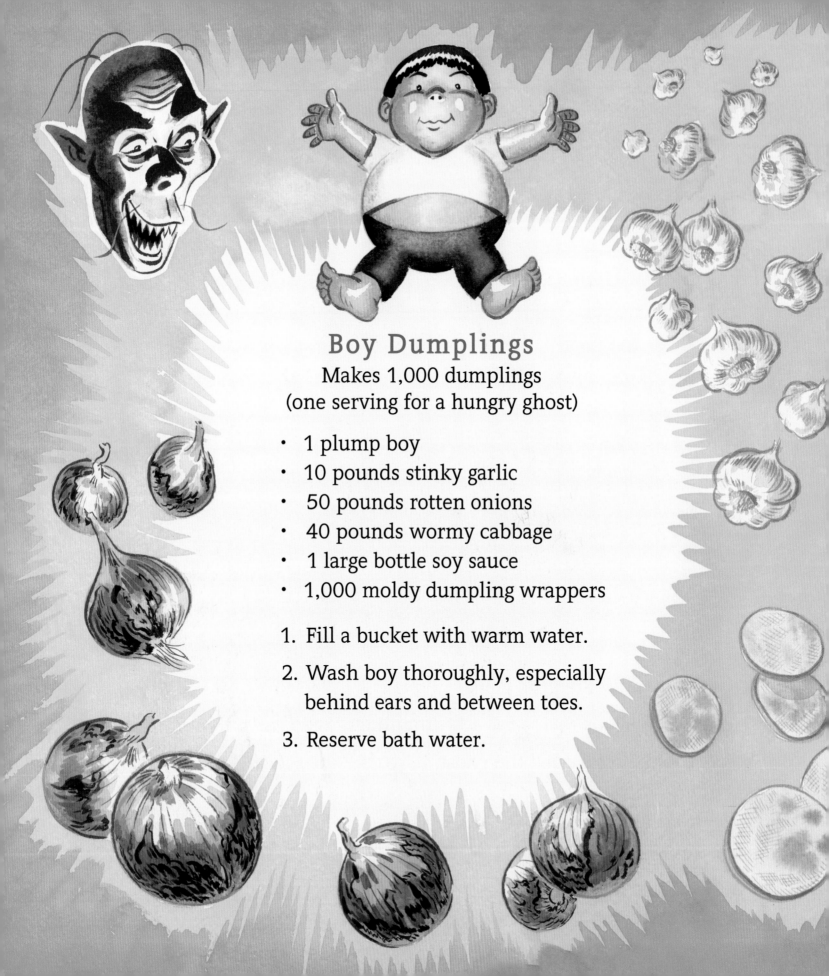

Boy Dumplings

Makes 1,000 dumplings
(one serving for a hungry ghost)

- 1 plump boy
- 10 pounds stinky garlic
- 50 pounds rotten onions
- 40 pounds wormy cabbage
- 1 large bottle soy sauce
- 1,000 moldy dumpling wrappers

1. Fill a bucket with warm water.

2. Wash boy thoroughly, especially behind ears and between toes.

3. Reserve bath water.

男孩馅饺子

1,000 个饺子（一个饿鬼的食量）

- 1 个胖胖的男孩
- 10 磅臭的大蒜
- 50 磅腐烂的洋葱
- 40 磅遭虫吃过的包菜
- 1 大瓶酱油
- 1,000 片霉饺子皮

1. 在水桶里装上温水。

2. 将男孩彻底清洗干净，尤其是耳根和脚趾。

3. 保留洗澡水。

4. Dry boy, massage boy's feet, and let boy nap.

5. Wash vegetables in dirty bath water. Chop and mix remaining ingredients. Gently wake boy with feathers …

4. 将男孩擦干,按摩男孩的脚,再让男孩睡一会儿。

5. 在肮脏的洗澡水里洗菜。将所有原料切好并搅拌在一起。然后用羽毛轻轻叫醒男孩……

"And *then* I chop you up!"
The ghost dashed out, barring
the door from the outside.

"接着我就把你切啦!"
说完,鬼冲出去,
并把门锁上。

Along the river he raced, in and out of stores, upstairs and downstairs, through restaurants, this way and that.

He had never worked this hard before, but he knew the boy dumplings would be worth it.

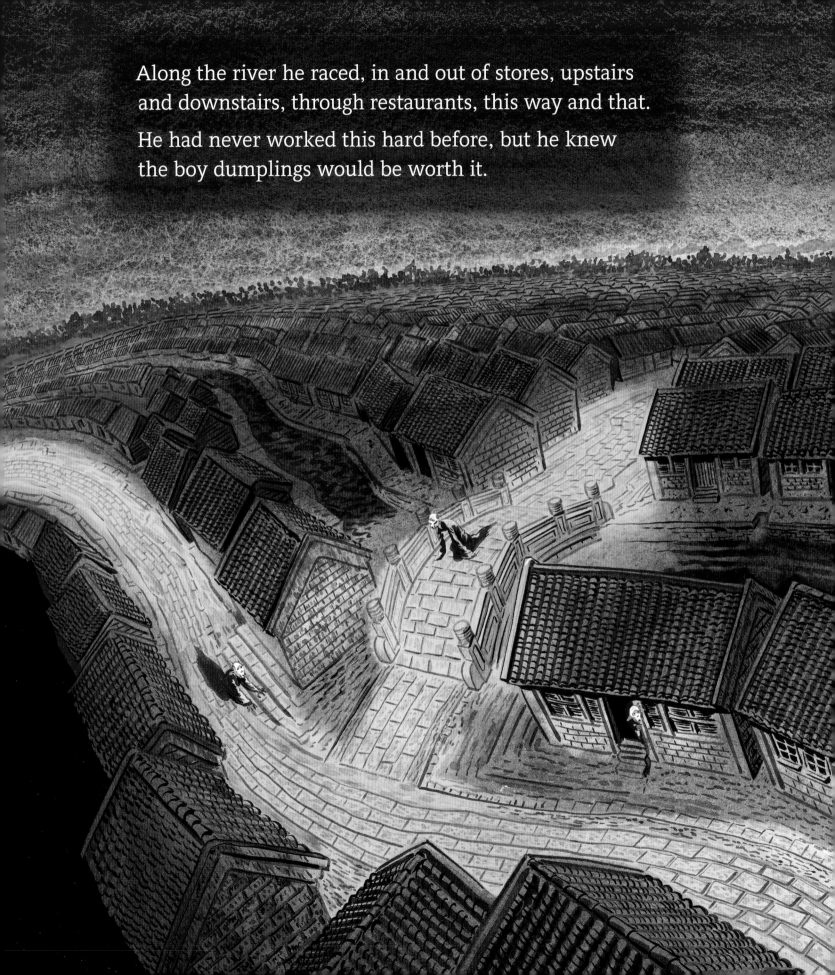

鬼沿着河岸,在店铺的里里外外,餐厅的楼上楼下跑来跑去。
他从来没有这么辛苦过,但是他觉得为了吃男孩馅饺子,
还是值得的。

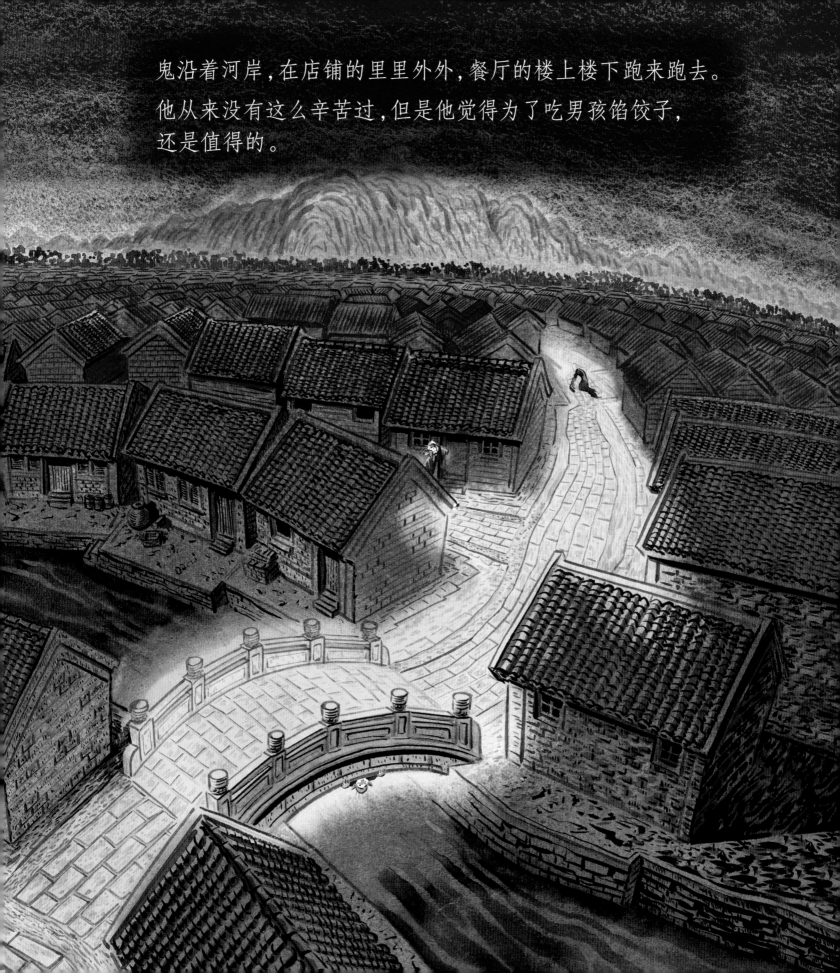

Finally, he came home carrying all the ingredients.

终于，他把所有的原料都抱回了家。

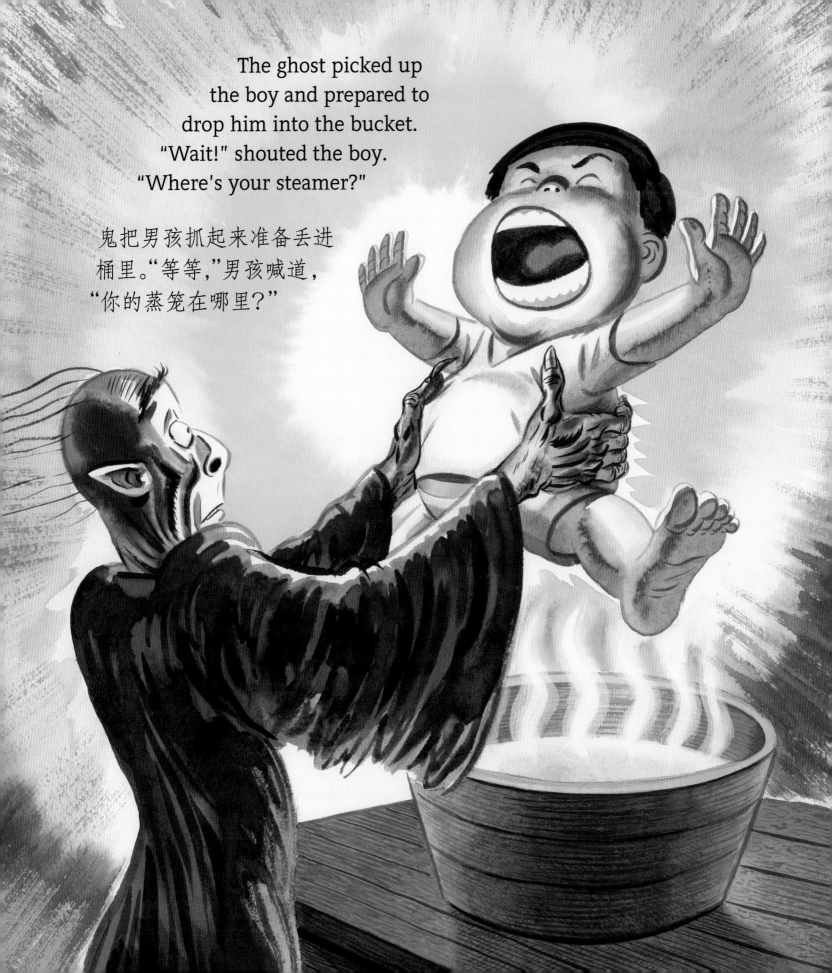

The ghost picked up
the boy and prepared to
drop him into the bucket.
"Wait!" shouted the boy.
"Where's your steamer?"

鬼把男孩抓起来准备丢进
桶里。"等等,"男孩喊道,
"你的蒸笼在哪里?"

The ghost groaned and dashed out again, running in and out of stores, upstairs and downstairs through restaurants, this way and that.

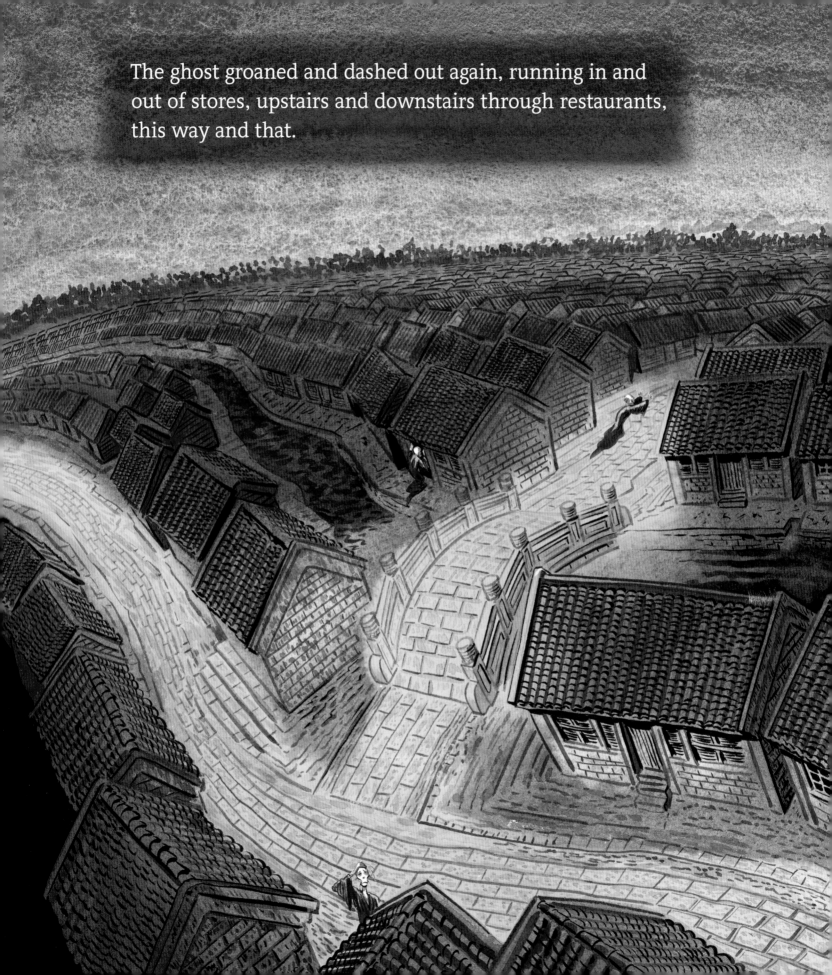

鬼的喉咙里发出了一声低沉的吼声，接着又冲出门外。
他在商店的楼上楼下，餐厅的里里外外跑来跑去。

In the city's biggest restaurant, he found a steamer large enough for 1,000 dumplings. Hungrier than ever, he rushed home.

在城里最大的餐厅，鬼找到了一个可以装下1000个饺子的蒸笼。鬼冲回了家。他从来没有感到这么饿过。

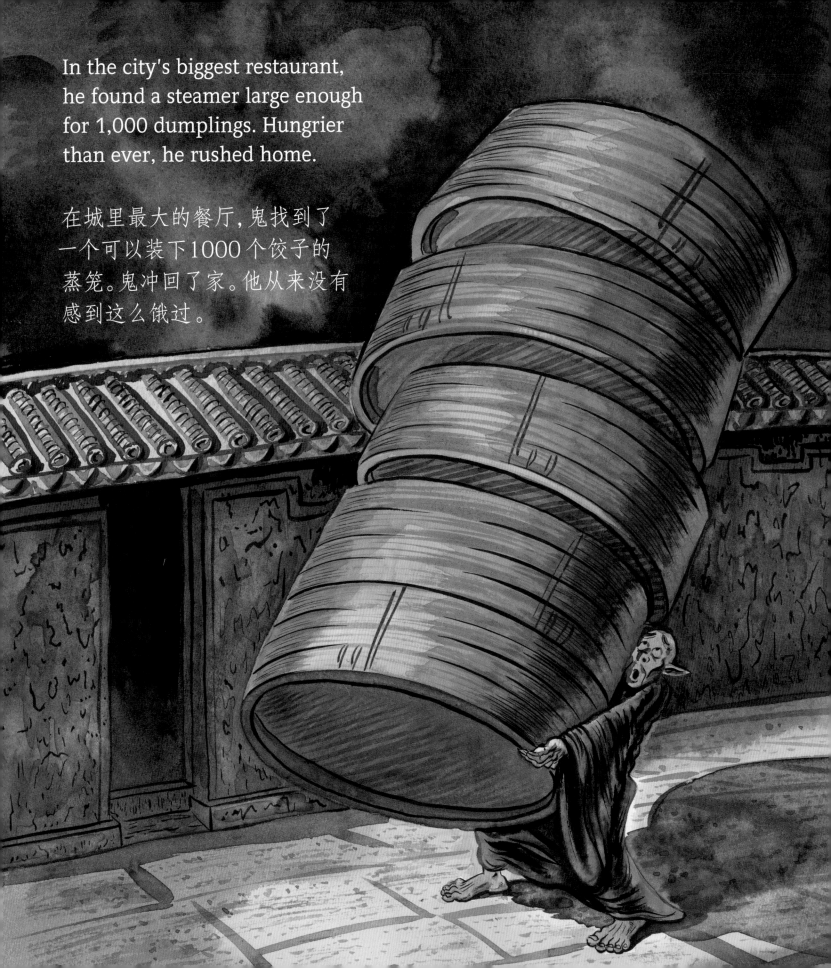

Carefully following the recipe, he washed the boy, paying special attention to his grubby ears and stinky toes.

鬼按照食谱要求，仔细地清洗男孩，尤其是他的脏耳根和臭脚趾。

Then he wrapped the boy in a blanket and set him down for a nap. The boy thrust his feet at the ghost. "Rub gently!" he ordered. "It will tenderize them."

It wasn't easy for the ghost to resist taking a bite as he gently massaged the boy's toes, one at a time.

然后，他把男孩裹在一个毯子里并安顿他睡觉。男孩用脚蹬着鬼命令道："轻轻地捏！这样脚会更嫩。"

对于鬼来说，要他抵制诱惑，只是轻轻地按摩脚趾而不去咬一口，真不是件容易的事。

The boy fell asleep, but the ghost had no time to rest. He washed the vegetables in the bath water, then chopped and mixed them.

男孩睡着了，然而鬼却没有时间休息。他用洗澡水洗菜，再切菜，然后又把所有的菜搅拌在一起。

At last, he was ready for the
sleeping boy. He tickled the
boy's ears with two feathers.

最后，他准备来处置这个熟睡
的男孩。他用两片羽毛去挠
男孩的耳朵。

"What do you want?" asked the boy.

"Time to chop you up!" yelled the ghost.

"Not yet! For the best dumplings, you must use fresh spring water for steaming."

"你要干什么？"男孩问道。

"我现在要来切你了。"鬼叫道。

"还不到时候，为了饺子好吃，你必须要用新鲜的泉水来蒸我。"

The ghost thought for a moment and then dashed out. Along the river he ran, over and under bridges, this way and that through narrow alleys. In all of Beijing he could not find even a drop of spring water!

鬼想了想，又跑出去了。鬼沿着河岸，在桥上桥下，胡同里前前后后，跑来跑去。转遍整个北京城，他竟然找不到一滴泉水。

Then he remembered the clear spring at East Mountain outside the city. Off he ran with a large jar. If he didn't eat soon, he feared that he'd be the first ghost ever to die of hunger!

突然，他想起在城郊的东山有清澈的泉水。于是，他带着一个大罐跑过去。鬼觉得如果不马上吃点东西，自己恐怕要成为第一个饿死鬼了。

Quickly, the ghost set the snoring boy on the cutting board and lifted the cleaver ... then something terrible happened!

The roosters crowed, and the first rays of sunlight streamed through the windows. The boy had opened the curtains! "Aaaaaah!" shrieked the ghost. "I need a dark place to hide! I am meeeeeellltttttinnng."

迅速地，鬼把正在酣睡的男孩放到砧板上，拿起刀……接下来可怕的事情发生了。

公鸡啼鸣了，第一缕阳光照进了窗户。男孩把窗帘打开。"天啊！"鬼尖叫道。"我需要一个阴暗的角落躲起来！我要被融——化——了。"

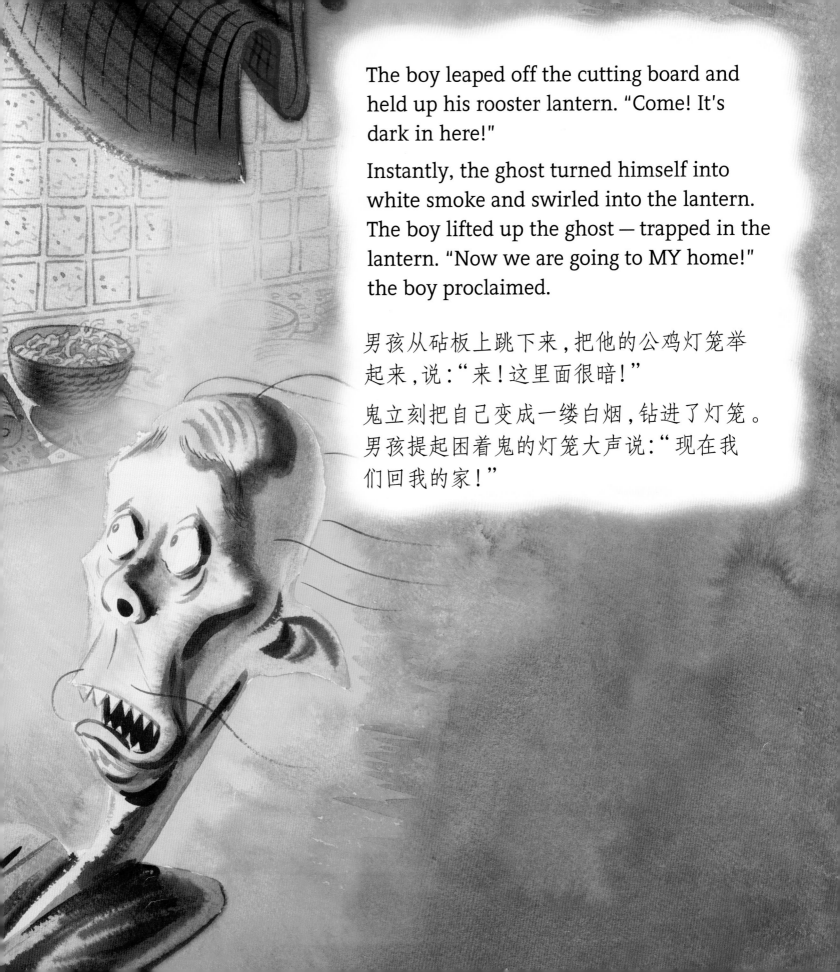

The boy leaped off the cutting board and held up his rooster lantern. "Come! It's dark in here!"

Instantly, the ghost turned himself into white smoke and swirled into the lantern. The boy lifted up the ghost — trapped in the lantern. "Now we are going to MY home!" the boy proclaimed.

男孩从砧板上跳下来,把他的公鸡灯笼举起来,说:"来!这里面很暗!"

鬼立刻把自己变成一缕白烟,钻进了灯笼。男孩提起困着鬼的灯笼大声说:"现在我们回我的家!"

The boy's parents were anxiously waiting for him. "Where were you, my dear?" cried Mama.

"I have captured the Garbage-Eating Ghost!" The boy proudly lifted up the rooster lantern.

"How brave and clever of you!" exclaimed Papa. All the neighbors came to celebrate and took turns peering into the lantern. They brought sesame candy, red bean cakes, coconut buns, and almond cookies. Together they cooked up 1,000 Boy-Free Dumplings.

男孩的父母正在焦急等着他。"你去哪儿了，宝贝？"妈妈大声问道。

"我抓住了那个吃垃圾的鬼。"男孩自豪地提起公鸡灯笼。

"你真是又勇敢又聪明。"爸爸夸道。所有的邻居都来祝贺，他们挨个窥探着灯笼，想看个究竟。邻居们带来了芝麻糖、红豆糕、椰子饼和杏仁饼。大家一起包了1000个肉菜饺子。

Everyone enjoyed a big feast under the rooster lantern. To this day, the boy lights the rooster lantern as soon as the sun sets, so the ghost hasn't had a chance to escape. Yet!

大家在公鸡灯笼下举行盛宴。直到今天，太阳一下山，男孩就点亮公鸡灯笼，所以，至今鬼还没有找到逃跑的机会！

Author's Note

The character of the Garbage-Eating Ghost is my creation. The inspiration for this story came when my son was about six years old. He was filling out just before another growth spurt. One night he was helping me making dumplings. When I saw his chubby cheeks and arms, I thought that if I were a ghost, I would love to eat dumplings made of a boy like him.

On the fifteenth day of the seventh month of the Chinese calendar, the Ghosts Festival begins. It usually comes in late August or early September by the Western calendar. It is essentially the Chinese Halloween. In some areas the celebration lasts a whole month.

The Chinese believe that during this time the gate that keeps ghosts out of the living world opens and ghosts roam free each night. They visit relatives and friends, and receive gifts and offerings.

When night falls during the Ghosts Festival, people leave offerings of food outside their doors. They toss sweet treats and dumplings out into the street in front of the house so hungry ghosts would not haunt the family.

In traditional lore, the ghosts would melt away in daylight. They fear roosters because their crowing marks the end of the night when all ghosts must return to the dark underworld.

作者寄语

吃垃圾的鬼，这个角色是我创作的。当我儿子6岁时，我有了这个创作想法。那时他正处在长身体的时期。一天，我和他一块儿包饺子。当看到他那胖乎乎的脸颊和胳膊时，我就想如果我是一个鬼，我一定会想吃像他这样胖乎乎的男孩馅饺子。

中国的鬼节从农历七月十五开始。阳历一般是八月下旬或九月上旬。这就像是中国的万圣节。在有些地区，庆祝活动长达一个月之久。

中国人认为在这段时间里，隔开鬼和人的鬼门关打开了，鬼可以在夜间自由行走。他们可以去看望人间的亲人和朋友，并接受他们的礼物和馈赠。

鬼节期间，当夜幕降临时，人们把一些甜食和饺子放在家门口的路上，这样饿鬼收到这些食物后就不会来骚扰他们家人了。

传说鬼在日光下会融化。他们害怕公鸡，因为公鸡啼鸣预示着黑夜的结束。那时鬼必须回到阴暗的地府。

Recipe: Boy-Free Dumplings

*(Have an adult help you with the cutting
and with cooking the dumplings)*

Makes 8 servings

Ingredients – Filling:

- 10 ounces ground pork or beef
- 4 cups minced cabbage
- 1½ cups minced leeks
- 3 tablespoons dark soy sauce
- 1 tablespoon sesame oil
- 1 package square wonton wrappers
- 2 large carrots, thinly sliced into discs

Directions:

1. Combine all the filling ingredients in a large bowl. Mix well.
2. Moisten edges of wrapper with water; spoon 2 teaspoons of filling into center of each wrapper.
3. Bring all corners to center; pinch together to seal. Place dumplings seam–side-up on carrot slices.
4. Steam dumplings, covered, for 10 minutes or until dumpling skins are translucent.
5. Repeat procedure with remaining dumplings.
6. Serve warm with additional soy sauce for dipping.

饺子制作

(在大人的指导下切东西和煮饺子)
8 人份

馅的原料:

- 10 盎司的碎猪肉或牛肉
- 4 杯切碎包菜
- 1½ 杯碎韭菜
- 3 汤匙的老抽酱油
- 1 汤匙的芝麻油
- 1 袋方形的云吞皮
- 2 根大的胡萝卜,切成薄片

方法:

1. 把所有做馅的原料放进一个大碗里拌匀。
2. 在饺子皮的四周沾上水;把两汤匙的馅放在饺子皮的中间。
3. 把饺子皮的四周向中间聚拢,捏在一起封口。将饺子有缝的一面朝上放在胡萝卜薄片上。
4. 盖上盖子,蒸饺子10分钟,或是等饺子皮呈透明色。
5. 按同样的方法做剩下的饺子。
6. 趁热食用,可用多些酱油做蘸料。

Enjoy more adventures by the Author!

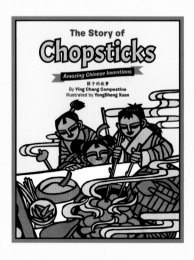

"Compestine concocts a delicious blend of fact and fiction... this charming tale [of *Chopsticks*] deserves a place in the multicultural curriculum. Xuan's richly colored traditional Chinese cut paper illustrations lend authenticity."
—*Kirkus Reviews*

"Traditional cut-paper art puts the wind in the sails of this charming story, appended with kite-making instructions."
—*Publishers Weekly*

"The trio of young cutups [return] for another Chinese culinary innovation... softly colored, cut-paper figures smile and stand in informal positions, reflecting the infectiously humorous tone. What will the young Kangs dream up next?"
—*ALA Booklist*

"Cut-paper illustrations are a fitting accompaniment to this amusing account of the discovery of papermaking. With bold black outlines and vivid coloration against a white, marbled background, the artwork captures the action as the boys exercise their ingenuity."
—*School Library Journal*